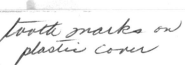

To Rosa, with love
−VF

To the memory of Isa Little (1913−1993)
−SH

SIMON & SCHUSTER BOOKS FOR YOUNG READERS
An imprint of Simon & Schuster Children's Publishing Division
1230 Avenue of the Americas
New York, New York 10020
Text copyright © 1994 by Vivian French.
Illustrations copyright © 1994 by Sally Hobson.
Originally published in Great Britain by ABC, All Books for Children, a
division of The All Children's Company Ltd.
First American Edition, 1995.
SIMON & SCHUSTER BOOKS FOR YOUNG READERS is a trademark of
Simon & Schuster.
Book design by David Neuhaus.
The text for this book is set in 20-point Albertus.
The illustrations were done in gouache poster paints and inks on paper.
Manufactured in Singapore

10 9 8 7 6 5 4 3 2 1

Library of Congress Catalog Card Number: 94-67870

ISBN: 0-689-80010-X

red hen
and Sly fox

by vivian french

illustrated by
sally hobson

Simon & Schuster
Books for Young Readers

Once there was a wood, and in the middle of the wood there was a tree. Under the tree was a house, and in the house lived Red Hen.

All the animals in the woods loved Red Hen because she was kind and careful. She mended and sewed for everyone, asking for nothing but a "please" and a "thank you" in return.

She always wore an apron, which had a pocket, and in that pocket she always kept a needle and thread and a little pair of scissors.

All the animals in the woods loved Red Hen—except for Sly Fox. Sly Fox thought that Red Hen would make an excellent chicken dinner.

One fine morning, Sly Fox woke early.
He yawned, and he stretched, and he
smiled, and he said, "Aha! Today is the day
I shall have my chicken dinner!"

Sly Fox hurried to his chest of drawers.
He slipped a pair of socks in one pocket
and a large sack in the other.

Then he ran and ran and ran through
the woods until he reached Red Hen's house.
Sly Fox knocked on Red Hen's door.

"Who's there?" called Red Hen.

"Why, it's only me, Red Hen," said Sly
Fox as she opened the door. "I've got a
pair of socks with holes in the toes, and
I wondered if you would be so kind
as to darn them for me?"

"Come right in,"
invited Red Hen.

In bounded Sly Fox. Immediately, he snatched the sack from his pocket and tried to slip it over Red Hen's head, but she was too quick for him. Up, up, up she flew, to the very top of the cupboard, where she peered down at him.

"Why, Mr. Fox," she said. "That's not nice. I offer to darn your socks for you, and you try to put me in a sack. That's not nice at all, Mr. Fox."

Sly Fox said nothing. He simply turned himself
around and around and around, until Red Hen,
watching him, felt her own head spin around
and around and around. She grew so dizzy
that she fell off the top of the cupboard
right into the open sack below her.

"Aha!" cried Sly Fox. "Home we go!" And he ran out of the house carrying Red Hen in the sack on his back.

Sly Fox ran and ran and ran through the woods, but the sun was very hot and Red Hen was very heavy. Sly Fox ran slower, and slower, and slower, until finally he stopped.

"Goodness!" he said. "What a fat Red Hen. I think I'll rest awhile." He sat down on a grassy bank and put the sack close beside him. He tied the top as tight as he could, then he lay back in the sunshine and shut his eyes.

"K'rrrrr…K'rrrrr…K'rrrrr…" snored Sly Fox. He was fast asleep. Beside him in the sack was Red Hen, who was wide awake. She was thinking hard.

"I'm wearing my apron," she said to herself, "and in my apron is my pocket, and in my pocket is a needle and thread and my little pair of scissors. Ho ho!"

Red Hen took out her scissors.
She snipped, and she snipped, and she
snipped a neat hole in the sack.

She tip-toed out. She looked
left and she looked right, she looked up
and she looked down, until she saw
a large stone.
She hauled the stone into the sack, then
pulled out her needle and her thread. She stitched,
and she stitched, and she stitched up the hole with such
tiny little stitches that no one would ever have known
there'd been a hole there.
Then she ran and ran and ran all the way home, and
made herself a strong cup of tea.

Sly Fox slept until the
sun went down.
"Ahoo!" said Sly Fox,
sitting up. "It's time for my
chicken dinner!" He picked up the
sack and hurried all the way home to his dark
old house at the very back of the woods.

"Din-din!" said Sly Fox as he pushed
open the door. He dropped the sack
on the musty, dusty floor, and built
a fire with sticks.

He took down a large pot and filled
it full of water. He put the pot of water
on top of the sticks and waited until the
water was bubbling and boiling. Then
he rubbed his paws together.

"Wakey, wakey, Red Hen,"
said Sly Fox, shaking the sack.

He untied the top and tipped the
sack over the water. The stone
fell in with a giant splash.

"Yaroo!" shrieked Sly Fox
as the boiling water splashed
on his whiskers.

"Yaroo!" shrieked Sly Fox
as the boiling water splashed
on his paws.

"Yaroo!" shrieked Sly Fox as the boiling
water splashed on his fine bushy tail.
Then he turned himself around and he ran
and he ran and he ran to the very edge of the woods
and out and over the other side, and was never seen again.

Red Hen continued to live
happily in her house under the tree,
and to mend and sew for all the animals
in the woods. She always wore her apron
with the pocket, and in the pocket she always
kept a needle and thread and her little pair
of scissors.